Acknowledgements: I want to give hon of his hard work on editing my books and creating my book covers . I appreciate it so very much. So for all of this and so much more I thank you Mark for all of the sacrifices you have made for me and our family down thru the yearsand I love and appreciate you so very much.

DEDICATION: I want to dedicate this book to my daughter , Natasha (Tosh) I love and appreciate you so very much .You have been so good to me down thru the years and you have went the extra mile for me time and time again. You are talented, beautiful and your kind and loving and you love to do things for others. For these reasons and so much more I honor you today.

Brutus & Chanel
Discover their First Christmas

The town called Snowy River was all a buzz with the news that some time before Christmas Santa was going to come to their town and pass out presents to all of the girls and boys who had been listening to their parents all year. He had a bag full of goodies and Santa and his elves had made them especially for each boy and girl who had been listening to their parents all year and had done well with their homework and school- work. Some of Santa's gift were not made by human hands but had been prepared with a bow on them to give to two lucky children. A boy and a girl would be on the receiving end of these two special gifts.

The town council was preparing to have the streets cleaned and all of the storefronts decorated before Santa arrived. Everyone was excited but especially the boys and the girls. They could hardly wait until Santa and his elves and reindeer arrived.

The Mayor was ordering his staff to have a gift for Santa of chocolate candy he heard that was his favorite chocolate peanut clusters, So he had his secretary go buy a 7lb box of that candy for Santa. The secretary, her name was Nancy, was asked to also pick up a lot of candy canes for the children who would be arriving for the main even. Which was Santa and his elves and reindeer. So much to do and so little time to do it. Santa would be here before you knew it.

Swish swash went the street sweeper as it was clearing the blacktop and streets of rocks and other debris.

In another part of town Sally and her mom was busy they was going to the dining section where the food booths were, because they were going to give out free food to all the kids and their parents who came to the event. Sally's mom was Genna and they were making cupcakes together but not just any cupcakes they were making lemon cupcakes with cream cheese frosting and white cupcakes with chocolate frosting. Lemon cupcakes had little lemon drops on the top of them and the chocolate cupcakes had a little Santa Claus on the top of them.

At the area where there would be dining and seating for everyone was where the food was being prepared. This was so exciting their town had not had such an important guest in a long time and they wanted to make sure they pulled out the red carpet so to speak and give Santa and he elves the royal treatment because it was not everyday that a town was picked by Santa to come and pass out presents.

In another part of town the school gardeners were mowing the grass lawns, Janitors were washing windows, the churches were having different boys and girls clean the sanctuary. The girls were polishing the pews and the pulpit, the boys were taking out the garbage and vacuuming the carpets and  wiping down the front doors. Eve020ryone is town was doing their part to help make their town sparkling clean.

Some of the moms were baking enchiladas, tacos and burritos with rice and beans. Other moms and their daughters were baking cakes, and pies. Some of the pies had homemade pie crusts for pies such as Apple, lemon, cherry and German chocolate cake, wow it was beginning to smell so delicious.

In other areas they were hiring parking attendants for those who would be needing to park their cars. They had some of the high school boys who would direct where they were to park their cars and to what parking spaces. Everyone was doing their part and working hard to make this event special.

There was several pets that frequented the town with their owners they were always a bowl of fresh clean water at the front door to the side of the door for pets who were hot could take a drink and cool of in the shade. The stores owners at several eatery places had outdoor eating patios and their dogs were allowed to come as long as they were on a leash.

There was a marching band with live music and the school's Christmas theme song was going to be played at this event. The town was going all out, and they were not leaving any stone uncovered.

There was a live band that was going to play several of the traditional Christmas songs as well as a few new ones the School band was going to March and play a song that they had been working on for awhile and it was going to be a hit from the way the

parents had reacted when their child/children had practiced it at home. Christmas is a festive time of the year and this was definitely going to be a festivities that everyone wouldn't soon forget.

After a late night of cooking food, deserts, and all of the setting up of the booths and cleaning up of the cooking and baking it was late and time to call it a night and take the kids home and get baths and go to bed.

The next day the sun was shining and the birds were singing and chirping and it was a beautiful day. The whole town had turned out for this day of festivities. About this time a loud voice booming and could be heard saying : " HO HO HO Merry Christmas!" Santa had arrived the children were heard screaming with delight.

The parents and were in awe of how beautiful Santa's sled was and with the reindeer all decked out in ribbons and garnish for the holidays it was a sight to behold.

Santa had the attention of the mayor and all of the crowd. Santa started to the middle of the street and he wanted to say He had two special gifts for two special people that had wrote him letters and now to answer their questions in their letters he had not and would not forget their special request. Santa asked for Steven and Ginger to come forward. Two kids about the ages of 8 and 9 came forward they were so excited to hear that Santa had received their letters. Steven had black hair and was grinning from ear to ear. Ginger had red hair and she was also grinning from ear to ear. When they got to Santa he reached in the sled and pulled out two

boxes. This one is for you Steven and this one is for you Ginger.Ginger went first in a beautiful box with a pretty bow on it was exactly what she had asked Santa for, it was a pretty white puppy named Chanel. She was a mini maltese and she was so cute. Ginger said, "Oh, thank you Santa I love her already." He said this is for you at your special request take good care of her and makes sure she is always fed. Oh I will said Ginger and she cuddled her little puppy and went to her seat to show mom and dad.

Next it was Steven's turn. He didn't have to be asked twice as soon as Santa turned to the sled for his present he turned towards Santa with arms wide open and said this is the best day ever!! Santa got a english bull dog and his name was brutus. Steven ran towards Santa and the dog and he just buried his head in brutus' fur. He was filled with joy that Santa had remembered that his other dog had died and he had requested another dog to love and call his own. He went over to Santa and hugged him and said thank you Santa this is the best day ever!

Next music started playing and the elves began to pass out gifts for all of the kids and people that had taken the time to come and then the festivities began, Everyone was eating, then they were dancing in the streets and taking pictures with Santa and his reindeer and with the elves too. What a party that all

of this town and the kids would never forget all of a sudden the music stopped and the mayor thanked Santa and all of his helpers and presented him with the box of candy. Santa thanked him and the elves passed our candy canes to the children and people began dancing in the streets.

Then Santa called his team of reindeer and they stood on their feet and Santa got all of his elves and with a HO HO HO & Away WE GO Santa disappeared into the night skies to make other children and their families happy and fulfill their wishes. Brutus and Chanel thought how lucky they are to have a family to love and call their own. And they all lived happily ever after.

Christmas List

1._____

2._____

3._____

4._____

5._____

6._____

7._____

8._____

9._____

10._____

Nice List

1._____

2._____

3._____

4._____

5._____

6._____

7._____

8._____

9._____

10._____

Mom's Gift List

1._____
2._____
3._____
4._____
5._____
6._____
7._____
8._____
9._____
10._____

Dad's Gift List

1._____

2._____

3._____

4._____

5._____

6._____

7._____

8._____

9._____

10._____

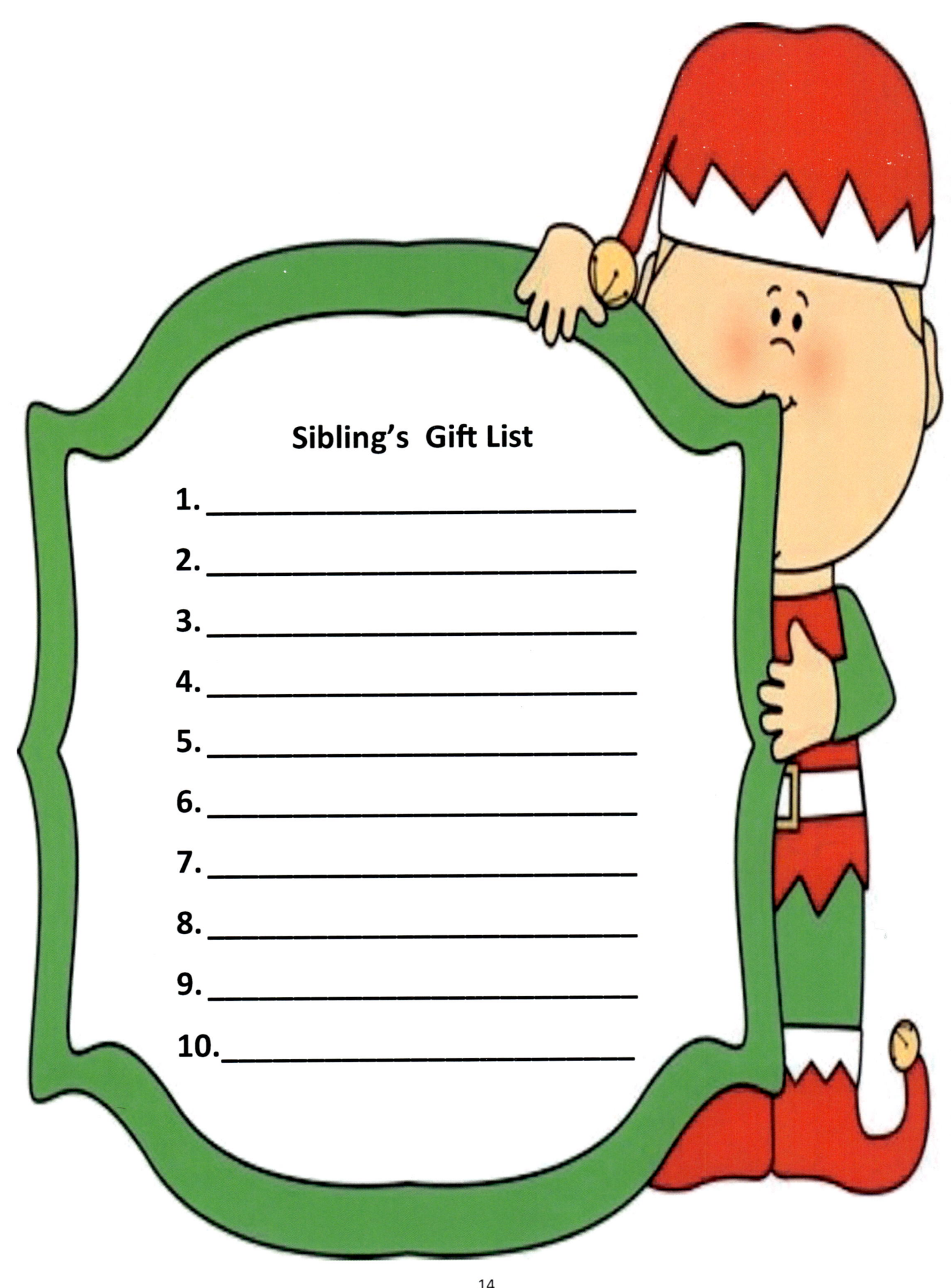

Sibling's Gift List

1. _____
2. _____
3. _____
4. _____
5. _____
6. _____
7. _____
8. _____
9. _____
10. _____

Santa & Rudolph are watching your coloring below

Santa told me to watch how you color me

Rudolph says, Color me with your best Friend

Can you add lights and bulbs

My box has some of your colors

Books by Teresa O'Keefe

1.The Unheard Cries of a Preacher's Daughter (Biography)

2. The Pool at the Bottom of the Falls (Fiction)

3.The Unicorn and the Magical Fairy Alisa (children's book)

4.Seeking Sunsets (Book on our travels to Mexico and Canada

5.Pinkie, Winkie & Stinkie To the Rescue (children's book)

6.Reflections of a Daughter's Love (fiction)

Made in the USA
Columbia, SC
16 December 2021

51705499R00015